PHOTOGRAPHIC ACKNOWLEDGMENTS

Women of Paris in Pictures first published in Great Britain in 2005
and in the USA in 2006 by Frances Lincoln Limited,
4 Torriano Mews, Torriano Avenue, London NW5 2RZ

www.franceslincoln.com

First published under the title *Quentin Blake et les Demoiselles des Bords de Seine*
by Gallimard Jeunesse in 2005.

Distributed in the USA by Publishers Group West

British Library Cataloguing in Publication Data available on request

ISBN 1-84507-624-9

Printed in Italy

9 8 7 6 5 4 3 2 1

Quentin Blake

Women of Paris in Pictures

petitPalais
Musée des Beaux-Arts de la Ville de Paris
PARIS musées
FRANCES LINCOLN LIMITED
PUBLISHERS

The Hand and Eye of Quentin Blake

A work of art lives only through the many different ways in which we look at it. If we look lazily, the work lies dormant. If our gaze is learned, it will stay trapped in the time and place of its creation. If we see the work from the point of view of strictly artistic considerations, it is the elements of content, form and colour which sing out. If our view is a poetic one, then the work reveals to us its infinite potential to evoke feelings, sad or comic reality, imagination ... in a word, humanity!

The way Quentin Blake looks at art is of this last kind. Because we admire the man and his work, and because we believe in his talent, the Petit Palais has given him carte blanche. Carte blanche to choose works from our reserve collections that he thinks have the power to charm. Carte blanche to salute our heritage by creating on the walls drawings that will charm our visitors. As a result the walls of our galleries have begun to float into the clouds, and the ladies of the banks of the Seine to talk, discuss, argue, laugh, cry, sing...

Now these works have definitely come to life for us!

Gilles Chazal
Conservateur général du Patrimoine
Directeur du Petit Palais,
musée des Beaux-Arts de la Ville de Paris

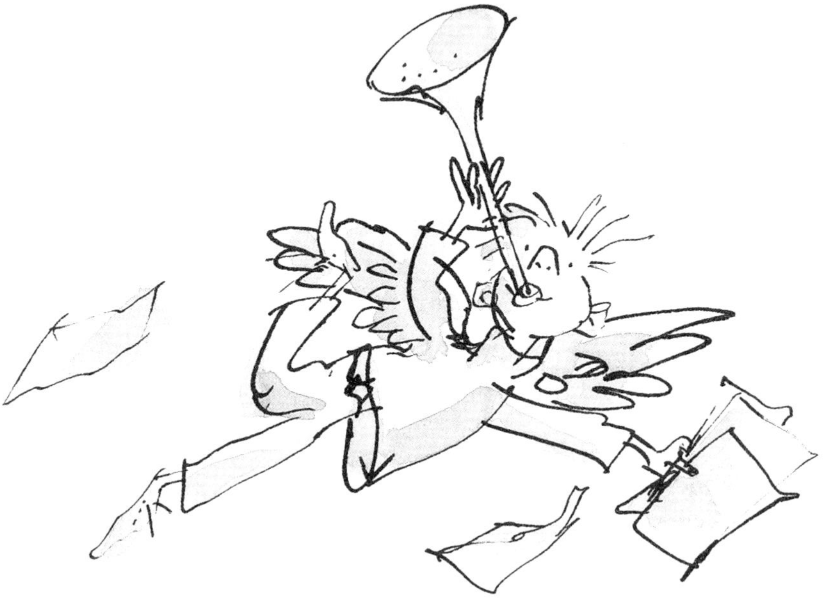

THIS BOOK ACCOMPANIES THE EXHIBITION
«QUENTIN BLAKE AND THE DEMOISELLES DES BORDS DE SEINE»
(December 2005 - February 2006).
THE EXHIBITION WAS MADE POSSIBLE BY THE SUPPORT AND HARD WORK OF :

Bertrand Delanoë, Mayor of Paris
Moïra Guilmart, Deputy mayor, responsible for Heritage
Christophe Girard, Deputy mayor, responsible for Cultural Affairs
Hélène Font, Director of Cultural Affairs for the City of Paris

Sophie Le Baut-Scherrer, Chief administrator of the Museums of the City of Paris

Gilles Chazal, Conservateur général du Patrimoine,
Director of the Petit Palais, musée des Beaux-Arts de la Ville de Paris
Maryline Assante di Panzillo, Modern Prints Curator
Isabelle Collet, Modern Paintings Curator
José de Los Llanos, Drawings Curator

Françoise Camuset, Scientific Director
Hubert Cavaniol, Exhibitions Coordinator
Aude Mouchonnet-Hendgen, Exhibitions Assistant

Virginie Gadenne, General Secretary
Sophie Adelle, Assistant General Secretary

Paris Musées Productions

Introduction

This book accompanies the exhibition of the same name which coincides with the reopening of the Petit Palais in December 2005. I chose women as the theme: women are there not merely in portraits but in many of the other pictures in the Musée des Beaux Arts de la Ville de Paris, especially those of the 19th century where the collections are particularly rich.

I can hardly express the privilege I feel in being invited to work on this project, and of the pleasures I have had in doing it. First, as someone who has been looking eagerly at pictures for most of my life, of encountering both little-known pictures by artists I have always admired and works by artists unknown to me, and second, as a practising artist, of choosing from such a rich diversity of approach and method.

I hope the arrangement in sections may help the reader make links and comparisons between the pictures. For me these works are interesting in that they reflect both social and artistic developments.

The drawings in this book, like the drawings on the walls of the exhibition, are all my own work. By contrast I would not have been able to do the work of choosing and arranging the pictures and commenting on them without the help of many people. The unflagging support and judgement of Ghislaine Kenyon, who collaborated with me at every stage of the project, were invaluable. We have both profited from the help and research of Barnaby Wright of the Courtauld Institute of Art in London.

Next the staff of Paris-Musées, and in particular Arnauld Pontier, Denis Caget and Aimée Fontaine, the Director of Paris-Musées. These are all new friends, but thanks are also due to my old friends at Gallimard Jeunesse with whom I have worked so happily for more than twenty-five years, and who have devoted their professional skills to the production of this book.

And of course none of this would have been possible without the generous collaboration of the staff of the Petit Palais, in particular Isabelle Collet and Maryline Assante di Panzillo, respectively curators of nineteenth century painting and the print collection. Thanks are also due to José de los Llanos, curator of drawings and pastels, and to Aude Mouchonnet-Hendgen, whose ministrations at every stage of the project were indispensable and who even found us our title.

Undoubtedly, however, my warmest thanks are due to Gilles Chazal, Director of the Petit Palais, whose enthusiasm for the spirit of joy and celebration which I have tried to make a feature of both book and exhibition has been an inspiration. A few years ago, I produced a picture-book *Zagazoo*, with a philosophical aspect which made it, I thought, suitable for adults as well as children. Its final words were carefully chosen and, as someone who at the time would never have imagined being asked to take part in this Petit Palais adventure, I hope I may be allowed to repeat them here: isn't life amazing!

Q. B.

INSTRUCTIONS FOR USE

To enjoy this book
you don't necessarily need to know
a lot about art and art history.
When you have looked at the pictures
with your own thoughts and
your own reactions you can,
if you want, find out more
about the works and the artists
who made them by looking
at the notes I have written
at the end of each section.

Close-up

Jacques-Émile BLANCHE *The Pink Hat*

Gustave COURBET
Portrait of Zélie Courbet

Marie BRACQUEMOND *Afternoon Tea*

Félix BRACQUEMOND *The Terrace of the Villa Brancas*

James Joseph TISSOT *The Newspaper*

Pierre PUVIS DE CHAVANNES *Four Heads of Women*

Paul SÉRUSIER *Breton Woman with a Bouquet*

Close-up

I wanted to begin with faces. These artists have chosen to take close-up views of the women they depict. Perhaps they are so close to them because they are not official portraits – you get the feeling that these are people the artists know well. Zélie Courbet was Courbet's (1819-1877) sister, and Marie Bracquemond (1840-1916), one of the few women in the Impressionist group and who was encouraged by Degas, has also painted Louise, her favourite sister. Louise lived with Marie and her husband the artist Félix Bracquemond in their villa in Sèvres and it is fascinating to discover that the Petit Palais owns a print by Félix Bracquemond of Marie at work painting Louise, an intimate view of their lives as artists.

Although there is so little background in the portrait by Jacques-Émile Blanche (1861-1942) it is still important as it manages to suggest so much about the life and energy of the beach and open sea, and the setting it makes for the lively and healthy face. This portrait was painted at Dieppe, a fashionable resort in the nineteenth century, where Blanche regularly spent his summers and the face is probably that of one of the Parisian models who posed for Blanche and his artist colleagues.

Paul Sérusier (1863-1927) was fascinated by the peasants of Brittany. In his painting of a young Breton woman, the table, the flowers and the woman herself appear almost two-dimensional, and the picture has become a pattern of cut-out shapes.

Pierre Puvis de Chavannes (1824-1898) was famous in the nineteenth century as a mural painter, producing large works for public places such as the Sorbonne and the Musée d'Amiens, and he was very influential with other painters of his time. In these paintings the people seem rather restrained and distant, and contrast with these studies I have chosen, which look closely at four women's faces and their individual characteristics.

The picture called *The Newspaper* is by James Joseph Tissot, (1836-1902) who was renowned for his amazingly precise depictions of relaxed moments in the life of the wealthy bourgeoisie... we can't look for insight into character here but there is no doubt about this woman's air of confident independence.

Seen from both sides

Aristide MAILLOL *Two Women in Hats and Study*

Aristide MAILLOL *Two Nude Figures in a Landscape*

Seen from both sides

This work by Maillol is one of the most curious and interesting in the Petit Palais collection: curious, because it is painted on both sides; interesting, because it tells us something about the practicalities of making pictures.

Aristide Maillol (1861-1944) first began a painting of his sisters, Marie and Elisa, wearing contemporary dresses and smart hats, but never finished it. He then turned the canvas on its side and used the blank strip to paint a small study of a landscape. Some years later he turned the canvas over and painted a scene of two nude women in a landscape. He then covered the back with another piece of canvas, hiding the earlier paintings. The pictures on the back remained hidden for over seventy years until an expert examining the painting removed the canvas backing revealing the earlier pictures.

Maillol painted the nudes in a landscape between five and ten years after he painted his sisters. They are in very different styles. He paints his sisters using lots of small dashes of different coloured paint, a technique known as *divisionism* or *pointillism*. The later painting of the nudes also uses strokes of colour but they are applied more densely so that the picture seems far more solid and bold.

The two sides show us that Maillol was able to represent women in two very different ways. He presents his sisters as elegant ladies of the 1890s, however, the painting on the other side seems timeless. Instead of painting from everyday life, he has created an imaginary scene, a sort of paradise, with women by a pool in idyllic natural surroundings. Their poses are quite formal like classical marble sculptures from ancient Greece or Rome (Malliol was in fact more famous as a sculptor than a painter). So perhaps he intended them to convey the sort of ideals we associate with classical art such as beauty, harmony and order.

Throughout the nineteenth century and into the twentieth, these two ways of representing women, either as real women from contemporary life or as imaginary ideals, occurred time and time again, as you can see from looking through the pictures in this book.

Into the country

Jules BRETON *The Woman with the Sunshade, Douarnenez Bay*

Jules BRETON *The Spinner, Douarnenez Bay*

Ker-Xavier ROUSSEL *Woman in a Striped Dress*

Into the country

Although he is not so well known today, in the nineteenth century Jules Breton (1827-1906) was one of the most successful and famous artists in France. Exhibitions often took him to Paris but he liked to escape the pressures of the city for the countryside and regularly visited Douarnenez. It was there that he painted these two small oil sketches of women on the cliff tops.

We might recognise the Breton costume of *the Spinner* from Sérusier's painting in the Close-up section. Like Sérusier, Breton went to Brittany to experience a simple and pure way of life. It may be curious that Breton decided to paint *the Spinner* from behind, but perhaps it suggests to us *her* view of the ocean, and the privacy and quietness of her remote country life. A quite different sort of person appears in front of the landscape in Breton's other painting: not a peasant but a sophisticated lady protecting her face from the sun with a hat, veil, and parasol. She is relaxed, but the yellow of her dress adds another note of excitement in the free and lively painting of the sea and sky – the sort of painting that can make you feel that you are really there amongst the weather.

There is a similar élan in *Woman in striped dress* by Ker-Xavier Roussel, (1867-1944) a similar pleasure in being out of doors. Once again the woman's striking costume is the element that gives focus to the picture; it, too, seems animated by the life that vibrates everywhere across the luminous white of the page.

Family life

Jules BRETON *Family Reunion at Bourron-Marlotte*

Berthe MORISOT *In the Grass*

Edgar DEGAS *Madame Alexis Rouart and her Children*

Mary CASSATT *The Bath*

Family life

All these four pictures have the air of being observed from informal, unposed everyday life, although in each case the painter has been very careful about the way the elements have been arranged. The painting by Jules Breton has the same spontaneous quality as the two pictures in the previous section. It shows the poet Théodore de Banville and his family. It seems to me that he is quite in charge of the women sewing and looking after the baby, even though he has taken his shoes and socks off.

The other pictures, all by Impressionist painters, show only women and children, in each case against a green background. In the pastel by Berthe Morisot (1841-1895) the adult, the baby and the child are a long way from us. We can imagine, if we wish to, what they are thinking and feeling, but my main sense is of their being buried in the greenness of the countryside.

We are much closer to the women and children in Mary Cassatt's (1844-1926) painting. Undressed or in loose clothes the figures gather together comfortably, surrounded by the green-blue reflections of the water. The strong diagonal of the shape of the boat and the fact that perspective seems flattened because we can't see the sky, reminds me of the enthusiasm with which the Impressionists looked at the Japanese prints which had become available in Paris at the time.

All the Rouart family of three generations were known to Edgar Degas (1834-1917) and he made numerous portraits of them. This pastel - a late work - although also on a green background, is composed in a very different way to the Mary Cassatt work. Instead of being piled together the figures curve outwards from the circle of the hat which has been laid in just the right place at the bottom of the picture – Madame Rouart to one side to attend to the demands of four-year-old Hélène while the nine-year-old Madeleine twists on her chair to the other. Is it just that she is now growing up that she seems so taken with her own thoughts?

On show

Paul-Albert LAURENS *Transvestite*

Antonio de LA GANDARA *Portrait of Madame Louis Rosenau*

Edgar CHAHINE *Midinette*

Henri CARO-DELVAILLE
Portrait of a Woman in a Speckled Dress

Léon-François COMERRE *Pierrot*

Auguste RENOIR
Madame Robert de Bonnières

On show

The portrait of Madame Louise Rosenau was painted by Antonio de La Gandara (1861-1917) who was a fashionable society portrait painter and the kind of person you would go to if you wanted to commission a dramatic representation of yourself that would impress your rich friends. Perhaps the painter's rather dashing signature was a way of telling prospective clients who to go to for their next portrait. Madame Rosenau wears a black evening dress with a high bust line and chiffon sleeves, set off by her red painted nails, quite a daring look for the time. However, the prominently placed wedding ring is telling us at the same time that she is also a faithfully married woman.

The portrait of Madame de Bonnières is striking in a different way. Her husband Robert de Bonnières was a novelist and critic and the painting was commissioned from Renoir (1841-1919), who was the only one of the Impressionists to make part of his living by painting portraits to order. What is unusual in the picture is the contrast between the restrained and modest pose of the sitter and the strength and audacity of the colours with which Renoir chose to depict her.

The sitter in Caro-Delvaille's (1876-1928) *Portrait of a Woman in a Speckled Dress* is seen in profile, like the Breton peasant girl in the painting by Sérusier, and somehow this pose allows her a certain discreet pride in her posture which contrasts with her patterned dress.

Transvestite is a different kind of presentation: this is a theatrical costume for a single special occasion, and one can admire not only the quality of the painting, by Paul-Albert Laurens (1870-1934), but also the style and elegance of the costume itself.

I doubt if Chahine's (1874-1947) engraving of a *Midinette* was a portrait commissioned by the young woman herself; however, I think that there is something satisfactory in the idea that even someone with very little money is still able to present themselves with a certain pleasure and panache.

In society

Joseph-Marius AVY *Dance Class*

In society

Joseph-Maurius Avy's (1871-1939) painting *Dance Class* was one of the first paintings bought by the newly created Petit Palais (1900). It shows young women at one of these events which were still held as late as 1914. The Dance Class existed to enable eligible young women to practise for their first real ball by dancing with each other under the guidance of older women.

It's interesting though to learn that, even at this time, according to a play of the time, teenage girls found that to have to dance with each other was «desperately boring»; what they liked about dances was the opportunity to flirt and discover the husbands of their choice. However, whatever their complaints, I think that Avy created a beautifully organised celebration of this innocent ritual, full of contrast and fin-de-siècle rhythms.

The Introduction by Georges Jeanniot (1848-1934) could hardly be more different. There seems to be a story but it's not immediately apparent to me what it is. I can't help speculating about the different roles of the three characters – the rather untrustworthy-looking young man, the impassive young woman – and feeling pessimistic about the outcome.

This picture is also of interest to me because I knew the name of Jeanniot – he was a friend and contemporary of Degas – but had never seen a painting by him, and it was gratifying to find it painted with such confidence and verve.

In the city

Constantin GUYS
Man and Woman out Walking

Constantin GUYS
Couple Walking

Constantin GUYS *Ladies of the Night*

Constantin GUYS *Woman with a Basket*

Félix BUHOT *National Holiday on Boulevard de Clichy*

Félix BUHOT *Place Pigalle*

Édouard VUILLARD
On the Pont de l'Europe

Édouard VUILLARD
Two Sisters-in-Law

Édouard VUILLARD *The Tuileries Gardens*

Auguste LEPÈRE *The Tuileries Pond*

In the city

The artists of the nineteenth century found a rich source of inspiration in the public life of the capital, its streets and parks, shops and exhibitions. The watercolour drawings of Constantin Guys (1802-1892) have an impromptu, immediate air about them which tells you that they are the work of a visual reporter of modern life (that aspect of Guys' work that so appealed to the poet Charles Baudelaire).

Félix Buhot (1847-1898) was also driven by an appetite for the life going on around him; an appetite so great in fact that it is as if he could not be satisfied with a single image, and any etching has to overflow into lively marginal sketches, such is the wealth of material before him.

The lithographs of Edouard Vuillard (1868-1940) take, with exquisite taste, a different view of the life of the time. The two students of *On the Pont de l'Europe* could later become, perhaps, the *Two Sisters-in-Law* in town costume. Of additional interest is the fact that we know who these young women are: Marthe Merlot and Misia Natanson. Misia was the wife of the director of *La Revue Blanche* – the magazine illustrated by Vuillard and his friends.

The same subtlety of colour and contrast of tone I have already noticed are present in Vuillard's *The Tuileries Gardens*, which you can compare with *The Tuileries Pond* by Auguste Lepère (1849-1918). Lepère was a gifted draughtsman who was a book-illustrator and also passionately involved in the development of the art of the print. I think there is something exhilarating about both the extraordinary skill with which this image is cut on wood and the strong linear rhythm that runs through it.

Félix Vallotton (1865-1925) was a member of the group of Nabis, and at this period he was known for his magazine illustrations and prints. These works, influenced by the Japanese prints and cut with a knife on wood, combine a simplicity of means with a sophisticated humour. This picture shows the vitrine of the fashionable jeweller Lalique in the Exposition Universelle of 1900 – or rather, wittily, the backs or profiles of the (mainly female) visitors crowded in front of it.

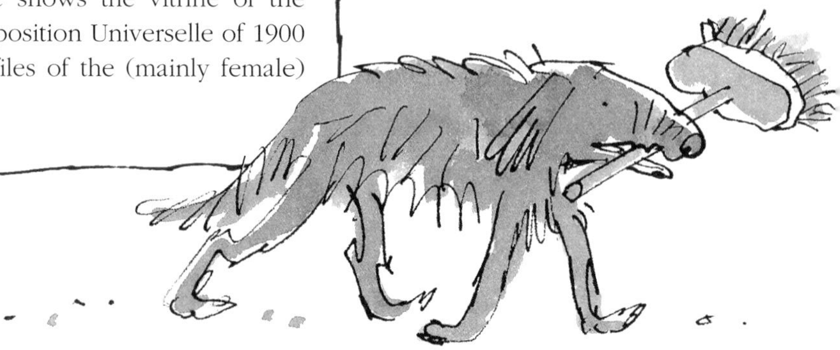

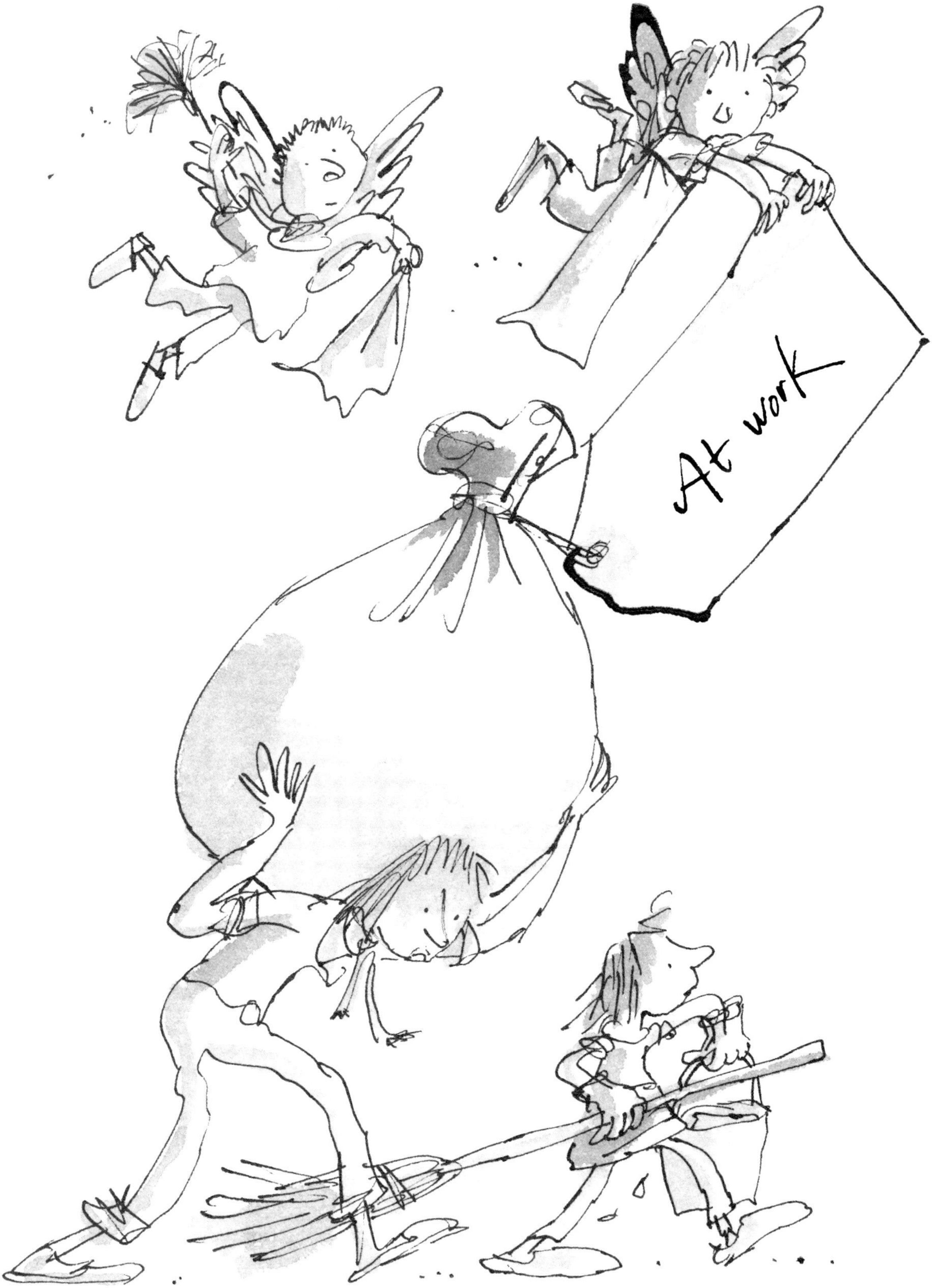
At work

Edgar CHAHINE *Winter Morning on Boulevard Ney*

Théophile Alexandre STEINLEN *On the tram, inside the stagecoach*

Théophile Alexandre STEINLEN
Laundrywomen : dirty laundry, clean laundry

Théophile Alexandre STEINLEN *Conversation on a Doorstep, or the Dive*

Édouard VUILLARD *The Cook*

Jean-Louis FORAIN *In the Wings*

TOULOUSE-LAUTREC *Émilienne d'Alençon Rehearsing at the Folies-Bergère*

TOULOUSE-LAUTREC *Nicole at the Gaîté-Rochechouart*

ON STAGE

J-L Forain (1852-1931) was a painter and illustrator who, like many of his contemporaries, was fascinated by the life of Paris both by day and by night. In *In the Wings* we encounter one of the fashionable men who at that time had access to the backstage world of the theatre and the extra-theatrical attentions of the singers and ballet dancers.

In addition to the traditional theatre there was coming into being a new world of places of entertainment – vaudevilles, music halls, cabarets – with an urgency and excitement for young artists, and a developing mastery of colour lithography to serve them. In the *Café-concert* depicted by Théo van Rysselberghe (1862-1926) we can see both the audience and the performer, May Belfort. She was drawn many times by Henri de Toulouse-Lautrec (1864-1901) who was a passionate enthusiast of the world of the theatre and of dance-halls.

He depicted many of the performers of the time, such as Yvette Guilbert and Aristide Bruant; the posters that he made of them not only became famous but have remained famous ever since.

These two lithographs by Lautrec are entirely in black-and-white, a rich deep subtle range of tones handled with extraordinary mastery. (Lautrec had just discovered a way of spraying on litho ink from a brush). One print, a rehearsal at the Folies-Bergère, shows the dancer Émilienne d'Alençon and the ballet mistress Mariquita (on the right) – a single moment of action wonderfully seized in flight. In the other the actress Nicolle is appearing as a low-class prostitute, but is made impressive – almost frightening – by being centrally placed on the page and by the dramatic lighting of the footlights from below. Both these powerful images are, in the wonderfully fluent work of Lautrec, the nearest, it seems to me, to the lithographs of Daumier earlier in the century.

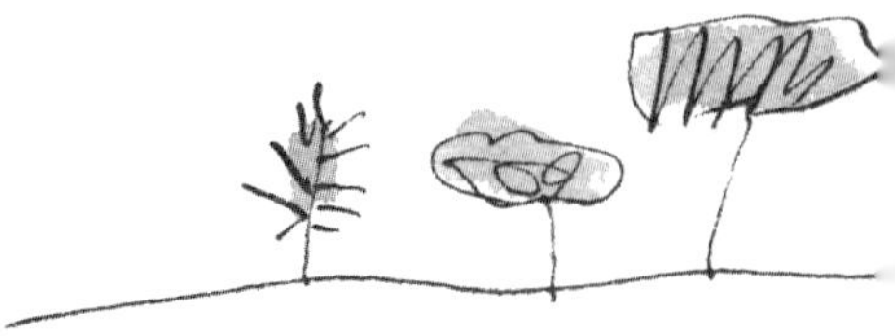

Out and about

Léon-François COMERRE *Bicycle at Le Vésinet*

Jacques-Émile BLANCHE *Mademoiselle Meuriot on Her Pony*

Out and about

I have always been fascinated by the importance of the bicycle in French life especially since it has it produced so many wonderful pictures. I was very happy to find a bicycle in the collections of the Petit Palais.

When Léon-François Comerre (1850-1934) painted this picture bicycles like this had only been commonly available for about ten years. From the 1880s onwards cycling was a huge craze; it was the most modern way to get around. For women especially cycling was liberating because it meant they could travel great distances cheaply and with ease.

However, I think that Comerre's painting doesn't quite capture this modern spirit of excitement and liberation; it seems more like a traditional portrait of a young woman who just happens to be holding a bike. But perhaps that is the aspect of the picture that tells us that the bicycle really had become part of everyday life.

Jacques-Émile Blanche's (1861-1942) portrait of Mademoiselle Meuriot makes a striking comparison. Riding side-saddle on a pony was a very traditional way for women to travel around, but Blanche makes it seem much less so by setting the scene in a blank space that has no associations with traditions from the past – it feels fresh and new. Mademoiselle Meuriot turns to look at us directly, confidently and without self-consciousness.

Mademoiselle Meuriot was known to the painter – in fact there was a long friendship between their two families – and, later on, this picture was given to the Petit Palais by the daughter of the young woman we see in the picture, along with several others.

Idyllic

Maurice DENIS *Evening in Florence - the Cantata*

Maurice DENIS *Evening in Florence - the Poem*

Maurice DENIS *Evening in Florence - Bathers*

Idyllic

Many of the pictures we have been looking at are of women observed from contemporary life. However, the women in these mural panels by Maurice Denis (1870-1943) seem to belong to an earlier age; and in fact these pictures were inspired by the *Decameron* of Boccaccio, in which a group of young men and women retreat from Florence to avoid the plague and tell each other stories in the safety of a palace with a beautiful garden in the Tuscan countryside.

Denis was part of a group of artists called the «Nabis», which is the Hebrew word for prophet. They saw themselves as the prophets of a different style of art that looked back for inspiration to the mural paintings of Italian artists from the fourteenth and fifteenth centuries.

Maurice Denis carried out a number of mural commissions, and the pictures we see here were created specially for Charles Stern – a businessman who was also a painter and poet – for the cupola of a room in his house in Paris – which is why they are this unusual shape. There were originally four of them, as well as four small paintings, but they were dispersed during the 1914-18 war, and it was only in 1937 that Maurice Denis retrieved the three we see here, and gave them to the Petit Palais.

Ker-Xavier Roussel, though also belonging to the group of Nabis and influenced by the traditions of classical art (surely these Baigneuses must be nymphs or naiads) uses in his prints a technique much more reminiscent of Impressionism; there is a lively juxtaposition of colours and an awareness of the luminosity of the paper.

Mysterious

Odilon REDON *Bust of a Woman with Arms Spread*

Odilon REDON *Studies : Woman, Flowers and Animals*

Paul Albert STECK *Ophelia*

Gaston BÉTHUNE *The Charmer*

Mysterious

When we look at these pictures I think we need to remember that some artists and writers reacted against the importance that the nineteenth century gave to scientific explanations of life. They preferred to believe that the world was full of mystery and wonder that could never be understood by scientific examination. It was in the idea of woman that they found the embodiment of much of this mystery.

Ophelia, in the painting by Albert Steck (1866-1924), is the young woman who, rejected by Hamlet in Shakespeare's play of the same name, drowned herself. Like other elements of Shakespeare's work her tragic fate fascinated many of the writers and artists of the nineteenth century. Steck's picture is particularly unusual because, instead of showing Ophelia floating along on the surface of the river, the artist depicts her upright under the water with her hair and garments swirling about her. I can't help feeling that somehow she is not dead but in a strange kind of trance in which she has become part of the underwater life of the river – yet some other kind of naïad.

There is a more sinister atmosphere of the unknown in *The Charmer* by Gaston Béthune (1857-1897). The darkness of the forest, the submissiveness of the animals as they gather towards this distant white-clad figure with her violin, everything contributes to a scene which stimulates the imagination of the viewer with a taste for the mysterious and inexplicable.

Almost every work by Odilon Redon (1840-1916) has something strange about it, and some are very strange indeed. I have to admit that I could not resist including *Studies* for its vivacity, although it is lacking in mystery by the standards of the other work of Redon – except perhaps for that bat-like creature crouched in the bottom right-hand corner of the sheet. More typical is the watercolour titled *Bust of a Woman with Arms Spread*; more typical even in the fact that I don't think we can even be quite sure of the gender of this androgynous figure.

This is the celebrated painting by Courbet that inspired the title for the exhibition on which this book is based. You will find it in the permanent collections among other great works by artists of the nineteenth and other centuries.

List of the works from the Petit Palais included in the exhibition

Joseph-Marius AVY, *Dance Class*, 1903, oil on canvas, 139 x 219 cm, purchased 1903 38

Gaston BÉTHUNE, *The Charmer*, 1895 oil on canvas, 175 x 131 cm, gift of the artist, 1895 75

Jacques-Émile BLANCHE, *The Pink Hat*, 1883, oil on canvas, 55.6 x 46.5 cm, gift of Marguerite Demaret, 1968 11

Mademoiselle Meuriot on Her Pony, 1889, oil on canvas, 223 x 227.5 cm, gift of Marguerite Demaret, 1968 63

Félix BRACQUEMOND, *The Terrace of the Villa Brancas,* 1876, etching 25,3 x 35,2 cm, gift of the artist, 1908 12

Marie BRACQUEMOND, *Afternoon Tea*, c. 1880, oil on canvas, 81.5 x 61.5 cm, purchased 1919 12

Jules BRETON, *The Woman with the Sunshade (Douarnenez Bay), c.* 1872, oil on canvas, 21 x 33 cm, , gift of Virginie Demont-Breton and Adrien Demont, 1920 22

The Spinner, Douarnenez Bay, 1870, oil on canvas, 23 x 27.8 cm, gift of Virginie Demont-Breton and Adrien Demont, 1920 22

Family Reunion at Bourron-Marlotte, 1857, oil on board, 23.3 x 31.5 cm, gift of Virginie Demont-Breton and Adrien Demont, 1920 26

Félix BUHOT, *National Holiday on Boulevard de Clichy*, 1 July 1878, etching, drypoint and aquatint, decorative margins, 31.9 x 24 cm, acquired with income accruing from the Dutuit bequest, 1988 43

Place Pigalle, 1878, soft-ground etching, etching, drypoint and aquatint, 24,2 x 34 cm, gift of Madame Félix Buhot, the artist's widow, 1908 44

Henri CARO-DELVAILLE, *Portrait of a Woman in a Speckled Dress*, c. 1910, oil on canvas, 75 x 51,5 cm, purchased 1957 34

Mary CASSATT, *The Bath*, 1910, oil on canvas, 99 x 129 cm, donated 1923 29

Edgar CHAHINE, *Midinette*, 1904, soft-ground etching, etching and drypoint, 46,7 x 25,7 cm, gift of the artist, 1908 34

Winter Morning on Boulevard Ney, 1901, etching and aquatint, 33.5 x 28.5 cm, gift of the artist, 1908 50

Léon-François COMERRE, *Pierrot*, 1884, oil on panel, 25 x 14 cm, purchased 2003 35

Bicycle at Le Vésinet, 1903, oil on canvas, 199 x 115 cm, Denyse Lion-Comerre bequest, 2002 62

Gustave COURBET, *Portrait of Zélie Courbet*, c. 1842, oil on canvas, 38,2 x 33,2 cm, gift of Juliette Courbet, 1909 12

Young Ladies on the Banks of the Seine (Summer), 1856-1857, oil on canvas, 174 x 206 cm, gift of Juliette Courbet, 1906 77

Edgar DEGAS, *Madame Alexis Rouart and her Children*, c. 1905, charcoal and pastel on tracing paper, mounted on board, 160 x 141.5 cm, gift of Robert de Galea. Estate of Ambroise Vollard, 1950 28

Maurice DENIS, *Evening in Florence - the Cantata*, 1910, oil on canvas, 218 x 364 cm, entered the collection 1937 66

Evening in Florence - the Poem, 1910, oil on canvas, 218 x 358 cm, entered the collection 1937 67

Evening in Florence - Bathers, 1910, oil on canvas, 218 x 362 cm, entered the collection 1937 68

Jean-Louis FORAIN, *In the Wings*, undated, pastel and gouache on board, 105,5 x 141,5 cm, purchase 56

Constantin GUYS, *Man and Woman out Walking*, undated, watercolour on paper, 31,7 x 22,4 cm, gift of Jacques Zoubaloff (Paris), 1916 42

Couple Walking, undated, watercolour on paper, 29,7 x 21 cm, gift of Jacques Zoubaloff (Paris) 1916 42

Ladies of the Night, c. 1860-1870, watercolour and ink on paper, 18,8 x 18,5 cm, gift of Jacques Zoubaloff (Paris), 1916 42

Woman with a Basket, c. 1860-1870, pen, watercolour, ink and gouache on paper, 23,7 x 16,4 cm, gift of Jacques Zoubaloff (Paris), 1916 42

Georges JEANNIOT, *The Introduction*, 1902, oil on canvas, 46 x 55 cm, purchased 1902 39

Antonio de LA GANDARA, *Portrait of Madame Louis Rosenau*, c. 1913, oil on canvas, 131,5 x 99,5 cm, gift of Bertrand Rosenau and Ariane Levery, 1973 33

Paul-Albert LAURENS, *Transvestite*, c. 1920, oil on canvas, 92 x 60 cm, purchased 1920 32

«Quentin Blake and the Demoiselles des bords de Seine»